BROOMS ARE FOR FLYING!

by MICHAEL REX

Henry Holt and Company   •   New York

To Karen,
for the whipped cream

Henry Holt and Company, LLC
Publishers since 1866
115 West 18th Street, New York, New York 10011

Henry Holt is a registered trademark of Henry Holt and Company, LLC
Copyright © 2000 by Michael Rex. All rights reserved.
Published in Canada by Fitzhenry & Whiteside Ltd.,
195 Allstate Parkway, Markham, Ontario L3R 4T8.

Library of Congress Cataloging-in-Publication Data
Rex, Michael. Brooms are for flying / by Michael Rex.
Summary: A group of young trick-or-treaters demonstrate that
"feet are for stomping," "eyes are for peeking," "mouths are for moaning,"
and "tummies are for treating." [1. Halloween—Fiction.] I. Title.
PZ7.R32875Br 2000 [E]—dc21 99-44493

ISBN 0-8050-6410-9
First Edition—2000 / Designed by Donna Mark
Printed in the United States of America on acid-free paper. ∞
1 3 5 7 9 10 8 6 4 2

The artist used pencil and Adobe® Graphic Software
to create the illustrations for this book.

Everyone ready?
Follow me!

Legs are for marching.

Feet are for stomping.

Eyes are for peeking.

Arms are for reaching.

Wings are for flapping.

Tails are for wagging.

Bones are for shaking.

Capes are for sneaking.

Mouths are for moaning.

Tummies are for treating.

Masks are for . . .

. . . tricking.

And brooms are for flying.

Happy Halloween!

M| Ⓢ 50| 4